# BELIEVE ME, I NEVER FELT A PEA!

## The Story of the PRINCESS AND THE PEA as Told by the PRINCESS

by Nancy Loewen

illustrated by Cristian Bernardini

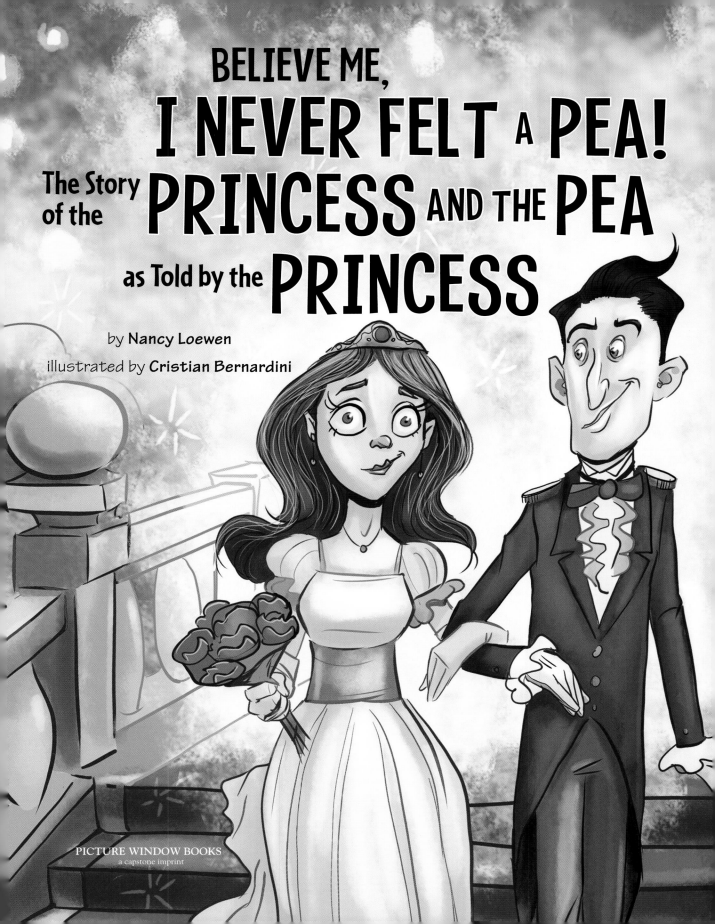

PICTURE WINDOW BOOKS
a capstone imprint

Special thanks to our adviser, Terry Flaherty, PhD, Professor of English,
Minnesota State University, Mankato, for his expertise.

Editor: Jill Kalz
Designer: Ted Williams
Creative Director: Nathan Gassman
Production Specialist: Jennifer Walker
The illustrations in this book were created digitally.

Picture Window Books
1710 Roe Crest Drive
North Mankato, MN 56003
www.mycapstone.com

Library of Congress Cataloging-in-Publication Data
Cataloging-in-publication information is on file with the Library of Congress.
ISBN 978-1-4795-8622-6 (library binding)
ISBN 978-1-4795-8626-4 (paperback)
ISBN 978-1-4795-8630-1 (eBook PDF)

Printed in the United States of America in North Mankato, Minnesota.
012017  010228R

# Can you keep a secret?

I mean a real lips-sealed-and-throw-away-the-key secret.

You can? OK, good. Here goes.

I'm not a real princess.

# SHHHH!

Yes, I slept on a stack of 20 mattresses. Yes, it was the worst night's sleep I'd ever had. And yes, I did marry Prince Matthew.

But there's a lot more to the story than that …

The first thing you should know is that Prince Matthew (Matt) wasn't all that interested in getting married. His dream? To be a successful businessman. He came up with one crazy idea after another:

Grape Plate
Berry Medley
Plum
Whip
Prune Surprise
Purple Cabbage
Casserole

turning the royal castle into a **hotel** ...

opening a **restaurant** that served only purple food ...

But the queen didn't want her son to go into business. She thought if he were married to a spoiled, pampered girl—a "real princess," in other words—he wouldn't have time for his silly dreams.

She traveled all over, testing princesses to make sure they were the real thing. But none met with her approval.

One princess politely ate tough steak rather than demanding a tender piece. **FAIL.**

Another princess carried her own luggage. **FAIL.**

Several princesses wore the same gown two days in a row. **FAIL.**

This is where I come in. And my dog. His name is Prince Super Pooch, or Prince S for short. Isn't that cute?

One night Prince S and I went for a walk in the woods. Suddenly—**CRACK! BOOM! FLASH!** A storm came up. We needed shelter, and I knew the castle was nearby. I picked up Prince S and made a run for it.

A maid opened the door. "Hi!" I gasped. "I'm Starla, and this is Prince S. Could we please spend the night?"

"Ah. Another princess," the maid muttered in an unfriendly way. "Follow me."

"No, I'm not a princess—Prince S is the name of my DOG," I tried to explain, but she didn't pay any attention. Maybe she couldn't hear me because of the thunder.

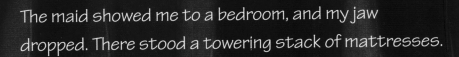

The maid showed me to a bedroom, and my jaw dropped. There stood a towering stack of mattresses.

**"Excuse me,"** I said, "but I don't need anything so fancy. Really, just throw a sleeping bag on the floor and I'm good!"

The maid sniffed rudely and left.

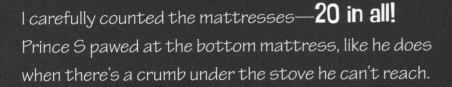

I carefully counted the mattresses—**20 in all!** Prince S pawed at the bottom mattress, like he does when there's a crumb under the stove he can't reach.

"Stop that," I said. "We're guests here. Be good."

The bed was super soft and very comfortable. The sheets were as smooth as silk and smelled like a flower garden. I soon fell asleep.

# But not for long.

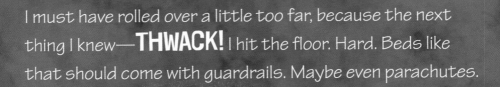

I must have rolled over a little too far, because the next thing I knew—**THWACK!** I hit the floor. Hard. Beds like that should come with guardrails. Maybe even parachutes.

I climbed back up the ladder and spent the rest of the night staring at the ceiling. I was too scared to move.

The next morning I was tired and cranky. "I hardly slept a wink!" I said. "See these bruises? I can't wait to go home and sleep in a real bed."

The maid stared at me for a moment. Then her face lit up. **"Your Majesty! Your Majesty!"** she shouted as she ran down the hallway. "This girl IS a real princess! She complained about the pea!"

So THAT'S what Prince S was trying to get at beneath all those mattresses. A pea! That ridiculous bed was a test.

"Again, Prince S is the name of my DOG!" I called after her. **"I didn't say anything about a pea!"**

But you know how fairy-tale weddings go. There's no stopping them. Beautiful gowns appear, the castle glitters and gleams, music fills the air, crowds gather ...

And suddenly there I was.

Married.

To a prince!

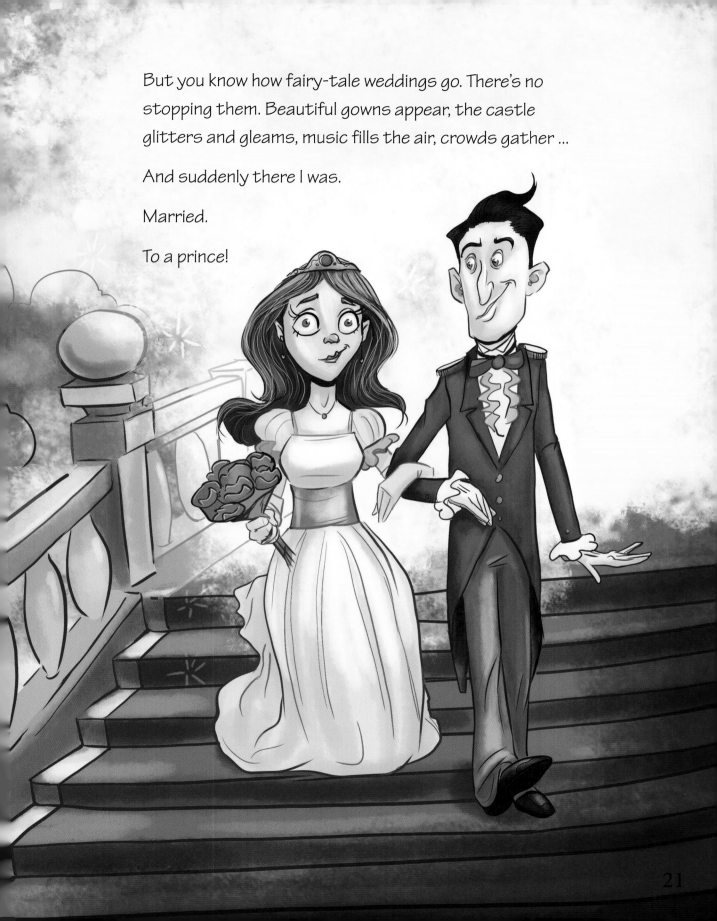

Luckily Matt and I love each other. And married life hasn't caused him to give up his dreams. In fact we're business partners. We've been very successful—**selling mattresses!**

Say YES to the best—a PRINCESS MATTRESS!

Have a ROYAL night's rest on a PRINCESS MATTRESS!

SALE

# Critical Thinking Using the Common Core

Look online to find the story of "The Princess and the Pea," the original version by Hans Christian Anderson. Explain how the original story and the version you just read are alike. Explain how they are different. (Integration of Knowledge and Ideas)

How do the maid's actions affect the plot of this story? (Key Ideas and Details)

Describe Prince Matthew. What information about him comes from Starla? What information comes from the illustrations? (Craft and Structure)

This story is told from Starla's point of view. If the maid told the story, what details might she tell differently? What if the queen told the story? How would her point of view differ? (Craft and Structure)

# Glossary

**character**—a person, animal, or creature in a story
**plot**—what happens in a story
**point of view**—a way of looking at something
**version**—an account of something from a certain point of view

# Read More

Engelbreit, Mary. *Mary Engelbreit's Nursery and Fairy Tales Collection.* New York: Harper, 2014.

Stewig, John Warren. *Nobody Asked the Pea.* New York: Holiday House, 2013.

Wilson, Tony. *The Princess and the Packet of Frozen Peas.* Atlanta: Peachtree Publishers, 2012.

# Internet Sites

FactHound offers a safe, fun way to find Internet sites related to this book. All of the sites on FactHound have been researched by our staff.

Here's all you do:
Visit *www.facthound.com*
Type in this code: 9781479586226

# Look for all the books in the series:

Believe Me, Goldilocks Rocks!
Believe Me, I Never Felt a Pea!
Frankly, I'd Rather Spin Myself a New Name!
Frankly, I Never Wanted to Kiss Anybody!
Honestly, Red Riding Hood Was Rotten!
No Kidding, Mermaids Are a Joke!
No Lie, I Acted Like a Beast!

No Lie, Pigs (and Their Houses) CAN Fly!
Really, Rapunzel Needed a Haircut!
Seriously, Cinderella Is SO Annoying!
Seriously, Snow White Was SO Forgetful!
Truly, We Both Loved Beauty Dearly!
Trust Me, Hansel and Gretel Are SWEET!
Trust Me, Jack's Beanstalk Stinks!

**Super-cool stuff!** Check out projects, games and lots more at www.capstonekids.com